Dusty

AN ORIGIN STORY NOVELLA

Valentina Iania

About the author

Valentina Iania is an author of small-town, cowboy, and spicy romance, making her debut with *Saddle and Bound*, the first book in the *Sunrise Ranch* series. Her stories are filled with intense chemistry, strong characters, and thrilling, sexy journeys.

Valentina's shared love of books began on her Bookstagram platform, where she connected with fellow readers before pursuing her lifelong dream of writing. You can connect with her on Instagram (@valentinaianiaauthor) and TikTok, where she shares her latest updates and writing adventures.

With many more series in the works, Valentina invites you to join her as she continues to craft captivating stories that will keep you turning the pages.

About the book

Dusty is a short novella that explores the origins of the Sunrise Ranch series. You can read it before, after, or during the main series, but it can also be enjoyed as a standalone, although it's highly recommended to follow the main series. The events in Dusty take place approximately thirty-six years before the first book in the Saddle and Bound series. At this point, Sunrise Ranch doesn't exist yet, and the events unfold at Lux Ranch instead...

Paola Lux has always hated Marco Riva. He's cocky, insufferable, and the one person who knows exactly how to push her buttons. But now, after years of animosity, something has changed. He's still a thorn in her side, but instead of making her want to punch him, he makes her want to... do other things. And that's a problem. A big, *dangerous* problem.

Because Marco isn't just her rival—he's her father's right-hand man, her trainer, and ten years older. Falling for him? Out of the question. Losing her mind over him? Apparently, inevitable.

Marco Riva knows better. He should know better. Paola is the daughter of his boss, his new job, and definitely too young for him. But none of that stops the way his pulse quickens every time she's near. It doesn't stop the dirty thoughts that creep in when she challenges him, the fire flashing in her eyes.

She's off-limits. He knows that. Yet resisting her seems almost impossible.

With stolen glances, sharp-tongued battles, and tension crackling like a summer storm, the line between hate and desire blurs faster than they can handle.

Tropes
- Age gup
- Enemies to lovers
- Origin story
- Second chance

"You dive me crazy"
"Then don't stop"
Alex and Rosie
-Saddle and Bound

Chapter 1

Paola

I'm heading toward the training paddock, just like every other day, when I come to a sudden stop.

I grip the fence tightly, my fingers curling around the rough wood. The air is thick with dust and sun-warmed leather, the familiar scent of long days spent under the open sky. This is my time slot —the paddock should be empty, waiting for me. But the steady rhythm of hooves against the dirt mixes with the uneven pounding of my heart.

I cannot believe this.

My boots press deeper into the ground as anger and indignation surge through me.

He's in the center of the paddock, every muscle in his body taut, perfectly balanced with the wild energy of the horse he's breaking. The bay rears up, neighing furiously, but he doesn't flinch. With precise, almost hypnotic movements, he speaks to the animal—not with words, but with his body. Commanding. Steady.

His denim shirt is unbuttoned at the front, sleeves rolled up to his elbows, revealing strong, sun-kissed arms. Beads of sweat trail down his neck, disappearing beneath the damp fabric.

I shouldn't be looking at him like this. I shouldn't feel this heat curling low in my stomach.

And yet, here I am, breathless, gripping the fence even tighter.

The horse fights one last time before surrendering. Marco runs a hand along its neck, and a shiver runs down my spine—like he had just touched me instead.

I hate him.

How dare he? Disappearing for years, only to come back and take my paddock when it's my turn?

I've always hated him.

Silence falls over the paddock as he turns to me, those dark eyes finding mine as effortlessly as if I were just another wild horse to tame. And suddenly, the fire burning inside me flares even hotter.

Some things never change.

He arches an eyebrow, looking slightly surprised. Then, he smirks—that same arrogant smirk I've always hated. That same damn smirk I've always found irresistible.

Not that he ever needs to know that little detail.

"Hey, Dusty. Long time no see," he says casually, as if nothing had ever happened.

I hate that stupid nickname with every fiber of my being.

My fingers dig into the fence one last time before I push away, striding toward him with purpose— chin high, gaze sharp, every step kicking up dust around my boots. But I don't slow down. I won't give him the satisfaction.

"I don't share paddocks anymore, kick-ass."

His grin deepens, sunlight catching in those dark, knowing eyes. He steps closer, crowding into my space, his scent—earthy, familiar, intoxicating—hitting me like a punch to the gut.

"Missed eating my dust that much, huh, Dusty?"

Chapter 2

Marco

The paddock. The horse. The sun warming the dust. The quiet. The solitude.

I've missed all of it.

But there's something else. A sensation. A prickle at the back of my neck. Years spent in crowds and chaos have made me hyper-aware when someone's watching. I turn—and I see *her*.

Seeing her is like a kick to the chest.

For a moment, I don't recognize her. All I see is a woman with sun-kissed skin, an athletic body wrapped in Wrangler jeans, and a red top that leaves her toned shoulders bare. The way she moves—confident, sure, dust swirling around her boots—keeps my gaze locked on her. My body reacts before my brain does.

Fuck.

When my mind finally catches up, the impact is even harder. My breath catches.

Paola Lux.

I can't believe it.

This knockout of a woman is the same fiery little brat I used to train with? Hell, I can barely believe it. And yet, there's no doubt. Same bright, mischievous eyes. Same golden curls—darker now, shorter. It's unreal how much she's grown.

She must've been, what—ten when I left?

The thought hits me with a mix of nostalgia and guilt. She was part of my life—maybe the best part so far.

Sure, the circuits were exhilarating. I lived my dream, rode the high of competition, won everything there was to win.

But *damn*, I missed home.

And hell... seeing her again stirs something deep in me.

Paola has always been fierce, sharp-tongued, relentless. Training with her used to push me to be better.

Used to.

Now, this is something else entirely.

And I *shouldn't* be having these thoughts about her.

But damn it all... she's *stunning.*

Short, wild curls frame her face, those blue eyes burn like fire, her button nose crinkles just the way I remember when she's pissed off. And her lips—full, tempting—

Shit.

And her *body?* Wow.

Lean, toned, wrapped perfectly in that damn top. And her lower half? An *actual masterpiece* in those Wrangler jeans that look painted onto her. Those strong legs, that *ass.*

A body like that should be illegal.

"Not a chance," she snaps as if she's read my mind, and I have to refocus just to remember what the hell we were talking about.

Fuck, I cannot have these thoughts about Paola Lux.

Not only have I known her since she was a kid, but I'm also *ten years* older than her. And if that weren't enough—she's my *boss's* daughter.

Antonio Lux has always been more than generous with me. He trained me, found me a sponsor—it's because of him that I had the chance to leave for the biggest circuits at twenty. And now, at thirty, with every championship won, I told him I wanted something different. To step away from the competition. To find joy in working with horses again, in a simpler way.

He didn't hesitate. He offered me a job immediately.

And my job is standing right in front of me. Just as stubborn and headstrong as ever.

"Still sharp as ever, *Dusty*?" I drawl, watching her face tighten at the nickname. "Hate to break it to you, but you *just* started sharing paddocks again."

Her expression is *priceless.*

This is going to be fun.

"What the hell do you mean?" she snaps, fury burning in those blue eyes. If looks could kill, I'd be six feet under.

I let the moment stretch, let the anticipation build. Then, with a cocky grin, I drop the bomb.

"I'm your new trainer. And I'm here to stay."

Chapter 3

Paola

Head held high, arrogant smirk in place, he shakes that annoying mess of brown hair out of his face. He's a little taller, a little more muscular, but other than that? He hasn't changed one damn bit. Same haircut—short on the sides, longer on top. Same cocky attitude.

Have I mentioned I hate him?

"I'm your new trainer. And I'm here to stay."

He says it with a confidence that makes my hands itch. He looks way too pleased with himself.

I laugh—short, dry, disbelieving. This has to be a joke.

"You've got to be kidding me." My fists clench at my sides. "Are you actually enjoying this? Get lost."

Of course, he doesn't budge. If anything, his smirk deepens, like he's savoring every second of my outrage.

Same old Marco. Same old dynamic.

Wait. No. That's not true.

Something has changed.

I'm even angrier with him now.

I never expected him to stay for me. Never expected him to come back, to visit. Never expected a letter, a message, a damn phone call.

Why would I? We were never best friends. To him, I was just a little girl. And I have always, always hated him.

So why the hell does this bother me so much?

"Still running your mouth, huh, Dusty?" He shakes his head, looking way too amused. "Hate to break it to you, but I'm dead serious. Now get in the saddle and show me if you've actually learned how to stay on."

My blood turns to ice.

No. No way.

This can't be happening.

I knew my old trainer retired. I knew I was meeting the new one today. But—not this.

My father wouldn't do this to me.

My heart pounds against my ribs. My hands burn with the need to hit something. Without a second thought, I spin on my heel and storm toward my father's office, kicking up dust with every step.

"Easy there, Dusty," Marco calls after me, his voice laced with laughter. "Wouldn't want you tripping over your own temper."

I don't turn around. I won't give him the satisfaction.

But if there were anything within reach, I'd throw it at his damn head.

My father is going to hear about this.

Chapter 4

Paola

And yet, I was the one who had to hear it from my father.

He made it painfully clear, in that tone of his that leaves no room for argument: *Marco Riva is the best there is. If I want to keep training, I have to do it with him. End of story.*

Which is why I'm marching back to the paddock, pissed as hell.

And of course, he's exactly where I left him— standing there with that smug little smirk, looking every bit as relaxed as if he knew I'd come crawling back.

Because he did know. From the very beginning.

Is it humiliating to prove him right?

Hell yes.

But what choice do I have?

"Well, Dusty," he drawls, *"if you're done throwing tantrums, we can finally get started."*

And then—he pulls off his shirt.

Just like that.

Now he's standing there in nothing but a white tank, and *holy. Fucking. Hell.*

I have never—*never*—seen shoulders this sexy in my entire life. Maybe it's the hormones. Or maybe it's the way those muscles are perfectly defined, sculpted like they exist for the sole purpose of making me lose my goddamn mind.

Dirty talk for my brain.

I swallow hard, my throat suddenly dry. My pulse? A wild, erratic mess.

What the hell is wrong with me?

Get it together, Paola. This is not a man. This is the enemy.

I take a deep breath, forcing my priorities back into place.

"Great. Then start by acting like a professional," I snap, my voice cool, sharp, focused on what matters: hating Marco Riva.

Not being turned on by Marco Riva.

"Otherwise, the next time I go to your boss, it'll be for a formal complaint—not for throwing tantrums, kick-ass."

His brows lift, amusement flickering in his eyes.

"Then I guess that means you can call me Mr. Riva." His smirk deepens. "Now get in the saddle."

Fuck.

I just lost the battle with my brain.

Fantastic. Amazing. Kill me now.

He looks away, and for a split second, something flickers in his expression.

Heat? Annoyance?

I'm not sure which—but if I had to bet, I'd say the second.

Because there's no way Marco Riva finds me remotely attractive.

And yet... I... I can't stop staring at him.

And the worst part? It's not even something new or impressive.

It's just him tightening a saddle.

A simple, completely normal movement.

Something I've seen him do a million times before.

But now?

Now, I see everything differently.

The way his biceps flex as he pulls the strap tight. The tension in his forearms. The way those veins stand out against his tanned skin.

A dangerous thought creeps into my mind.

I need to fix this. *Fast.*

Because Marco Riva cannot—*must not*—become my fantasy.

Chapter 5

Marco

"That means, as of now, you'll call me Mr. Riva. Now get on."
"Yes, Mr. Riva."
Fuck.
I can't stop thinking about it.
Not even hours later.
Not even now, as I sit here jerking off in the living room of the guesthouse Antonio and Silvia assigned me.
The guesthouse that's dangerously close to Paola's cabin.
It was hot as hell.
Christ, how badly I wanted to spank her for misbehaving. For being such a brat. For that damned way she provokes me without even realizing it.
And that perfect ass, swaying rhythmically in the saddle as she kept repeating that fucking *"Yes, Mr. Riva"* in that sugary, venomous voice of hers?
Fuck me, I was so jealous of that horse.
Did I wish she were riding me instead? Absolutely.
Did I want that spoiled little pussy on me? To feel her grinding against me?
Fuck.
Right now, I don't give a damn that she's younger.
That I'm her instructor.
That this is all kinds of wrong.
I just want her.

I want to hear her call me *Mr. Riva* again.

I come for the third time.

And for the third time, I spill a river of cum.

I collapse back against the couch, head thrown back, eyes shut.

I'm exhausted, drained—but I still want her.

I'm floating somewhere outside of reality when I hear a sound to my left.

I turn sharply.

I freeze, my heart slamming against my ribs.

The door is open.

And standing in the doorway is her.

Paola.

For a moment, I can't tell if she's real or just another sick fantasy conjured by my twisted mind.

I don't even stop to consider which would be worse.

Then the world stops.

And I realize—she's real.

Wide eyes. Parted lips, caught between shock and... something else. Her chest rising and falling in uneven breaths.

Her pupils are dilated.

Her cheeks are burning.

And I see the exact moment her gaze drops.

Fuck.

I should move. I should say something. I should pull up my jeans, cover myself, come up with some kind of fucking explanation.

But I don't.

I stay right there, arm draped over the couch, breath ragged, cock still throbbing.

And she doesn't look away.

A shiver runs down my spine.

My brain tells me this is a massive mistake—that I should stop, that I should put a line between us.

But my body is saying something entirely different.

Paola swallows. Her tongue flicks over her lower lip, wetting it.

Oh, fuck no.

A low growl rumbles in my throat—something primal, predatory.

She takes a step back.

I start to rise.

She should run.

I should stop.

Neither of us moves.

The fire in my gut hasn't gone out. It's turned into pure, consuming hell.

The silence between us is thick, electric. I can almost hear it crackling in the air.

I should pull myself together. I should—anything but what my body is screaming at me to do.

Instead, I tilt my head and lock eyes with her.

She flushes but doesn't turn away. Doesn't move. Doesn't run.

Holy fucking hell.

I inhale slowly, trying to rein myself in. "See something you like, Dusty?"

Her throat bobs with a shaky breath. Then she lifts her chin, stubborn as ever. "You're disgusting."

I smirk. "And yet you're still standing there."

Another shaky breath.

Her chest rises and falls in a rhythm that drives me insane.

Those jeans hugging her curves, that tiny top leaving her shoulders bare—Christ. I should stop before it's too late.

But then I hear it.

Her voice, lower this time. "What if I stayed?"

A bolt of heat shoots through me, brutal and uncontrollable.

I could press her against the door. I could make her take back every ounce of that defiance. I could have her right here, right now.

But then what?

My jaw clenches. I force myself to stay clear-headed.

"You won't stay."

"And if I did?"

Fuck. Fuck. Fuck.

I move without thinking, giving her no time to react.

In an instant, I'm in front of her. Too close. Her back grazes the wooden door.

I plant a hand beside her head and lean in, close enough to feel her unsteady breath.

"Dusty..." My voice is low, almost a growl. "You don't want to play this game with me."

She doesn't move. Doesn't speak.

But I can see the frantic pulse in her throat.

I smirk, slow and deliberate.

Then I pull away.

I zip up my jeans and walk past her like nothing happened.

"Go to bed, Paola."

I hear her sharp inhale.

Then, as the door clicks shut behind her, I let out a long, heavy breath.

Christ.

I'm so fucking screwed.

Chapter 6

Paola

I turn and run.

Not even a second passes after the door clicks shut.

I can't stay. I can't let myself breathe in another lungful of air laced with him—his heat, his scent.

Gravel crunches under my hurried steps. The night air is cool, but I'm burning. My heart pounds in my ears, thrums in my temples, tightens my throat.

What the hell did I just do?

I practically offered myself to him.

To Marco Riva.

The man I've always hated. The man who's always looked down on me with that smug, infuriating smirk.

And tonight, I looked at him from a very different angle.

My brain was already wrecked from what happened this morning.

But now?

Shit.

Shit.

Shit.

I take the path at almost a run, fists clenched, legs shaking with frustration. The cabin is just ahead. I slam it shut and press my back against the wood, dragging in ragged, uneven breaths.

I hate him.

I hate him.

I hate myself.

I hate the way I melted, the way my body responded as if it had been wired to crave him.

And I hate even more that he didn't give in.

Why didn't he? Why did he let me see him like that, see everything, only to push me away with a half-smile and a damn order, like I was some stubborn little girl?

Go to bed, Paola.

His voice detonates in my head.

A shiver runs down my spine, but it's not just anger.

It's something else.

Goddamn it.

I shove off the door, rip my top over my head with a growl, kick off my boots, peel off my jeans and fling them away like they're contaminated.

A shower. I need a shower.

Cold.

Ice cold.

I storm across the room, yank open the stall, crank the faucet, and step under the water without a second thought.

A freezing jolt hits me.

My breath catches, my skin tightens—but not enough to put out the fire raging inside me.

Because it's not just anger I feel.

It's not just humiliation.

It's desire.

Raw, clawing, unbearable. It coils low in my belly, pulses under my skin, makes me grit my teeth to keep from moaning.

The water slides over me—down my breasts, along my thighs, across my spine as it arches with the memory of what I saw.

His hands. His arms, tense and straining, muscles corded tight, veins standing out against his bronzed skin.

And that sound. That low, guttural growl of a man barely holding himself together.

A shudder wracks through me. Heat licks up my spine, sparks deep in my core.

No.

I shove my wet hair back, clench my fists, breathe hard.

I can't want him.

I can't let this consume me.

The icy stream pours over me, relentless, numbing.

And I let it.

Because it's the only thing that can drown out what Marco Riva ignited inside me.

At least for tonight.

Chapter 7

Paola

"Slept well, Miss Lux?" he asks, tilting his head slightly and adjusting his cowboy hat.

Oh, so we're back to playing games.

Bastard.

I clench my jaw. "Perfectly."

His smile stretches, slow and shameless. "Really? You seem a little... tense."

Tense? I'm a goddamn coiled spring, ready to snap. But I won't give him that satisfaction.

I lift my chin. "Shall we begin?"

Marco nods and hands me the helmet. His finger barely brushes the back of my hand as I take it... I really need to do something about this because even that brief touch sends a shiver down my spine.

I settle into the saddle, trying to ignore his gaze, which follows me like a shadow.

"Good," he says, his voice low, almost lazy. "Let's see if you can stay steady in the saddle today."

Something in the way he says it makes my stomach tighten. But I don't have time to dwell on it because he's already next to me, hands on the reins, his eyes locked onto mine.

"Squeeze your thighs, Dusty."

Oh, son of a bitch.

My breath catches just for a second. My brain knows it's a standard command, exactly what you'd tell any rider to improve their balance.

But his voice. The way he said it.

It's not just a command.

It's a goddamn provocation.

He watches me, waiting for a reaction. I force myself not to give him one.

"Like this, Mr. Riva?" I ask innocently, pressing my legs tighter against the horse's sides.

His eyes glint, dark and amused. Then he smiles, tilting his head. "Good girl."

Holy hell.

The training continues, and I'd love to say the tension fades, but that would be a lie.

Every damn command sounds dirty coming from his lips.

"Loosen up, Dusty."

"Don't tense up."

"You need to let go."

He's toying with me. He knows it. I know it. But there's not a damn thing I can do about it.

His voice follows my every movement, warm, alluring. The tone is always just a little too low, the gaze always just a little too attentive.

And the problem?

The problem is my body reacts.

The problem is that now, with my thighs clenched, my breath short, and him watching me from the ground with that half-smirk, I feel like I'm about to lose my damn mind.

"You seem distracted, Dusty."

His voice lashes through me like a whip.

I look down at him from the saddle, my skin burning, my teeth clenched. "I'm not distracted."

His eyes glint with something dark, something amused. "No?"

I move closer, slowing my horse until I stop right in front of him. Lower my gaze to glare at him. "No."

Silence.

Marco studies me, lips curled just slightly, those damn hands rolling up the sleeves of his shirt.

The same hands that, last night, were wrapped around his cock.

And I can't stop thinking about it.

I think he knows that by now.

Damn it.

Then he steps closer, so near that I could reach out and touch him if I wanted.

He tilts his head. "Good."

A shiver runs down my spine.

He notices.

Oh, fuck.

His gaze drifts down my throat, my chest, to my hands gripping the reins. Then back up to my eyes, and for a moment, I see exactly what he's thinking.

And it has nothing to do with horses.

The tension between us is a stretched wire—one wrong move, and it'll snap.

And just like that, he pulls back.

Takes a step back, runs a hand through his hair, his smirk turning cocky again.

"That's it for today."

My heart stops. "What?"

He looks at me, raises an eyebrow. "You heard me. Dismount."

I... fuck!

I want to kill him.

Kiss him.

Punch him.

But most of all, I want to put as much distance between us as possible and forget he even exists.

Only that's not fucking possible.

Who am I kidding?

If I haven't forgotten him in all the time he was gone... how the hell could I do it now?

I grit my teeth, slide off the horse, and as I walk past him, I brush against his shoulder on purpose.

I hear his breath hitch for just a second.

But then his voice follows me, soft, insidious.

"See you tomorrow, Dusty."

My body is on fire, but I don't give him the satisfaction. I keep walking.

What the hell are you playing at, Marco Riva?

It's pretty damn clear you don't want me.

So why the hell are you still a thorn in my side?

I need to do something to get him out of my head.

I need to get a grip.

Chapter 8

Marco

Christ, when she brushed against me with her shoulder...
I almost lost my damn mind.
I drag my tongue over my lips, dry as the desert.
Last night, she looked at me like she wanted me on my knees for her.
This morning, she looked at me like she wanted to tear my eyes out.
And I have never wanted anything more in my life.
But I can't afford this.
And the way she obeys my orders—insolent, defiant—I fucking lost it.
I had to send her away.
I can't let myself want her the way I do right now.
Because this is fucking madness.
I clench my teeth and turn sharply, a knot tightening in my throat, pressing against my chest.
The desire inside me pulses like a damn curse, an unbearable fire eating me alive.
I have to put it out.
I grab the lead of the ranch's wildest stallion, preparing to break him in.
My breath pushes hard through my nostrils, my blood pounds in my temples as I grip the rope and watch him.
Dark eyes. Wild. Unbreakable.
He moves nervously, muscles twitching beneath his sleek coat.

I see the same fire in him that's burning in me.

The same dangerous energy.

And maybe that's why I choose him.

I meet his gaze head-on. Let him fight—kick, rear, thrash against me.

I let him struggle.

Because that's exactly what I want to do.

I want to shake off this tension.

I want to rid myself of this insane need to have Paola beneath me, above me, against me.

And if I can't do it with her, I'll do it here.

With a swift motion, I pull the rope just enough to remind him who's in control.

My muscles scream, arms locked against his force, legs planted firmly as the weight of the beast tries to drag me down.

Spoiler alert: I won't fall.

He thrashes again, neighs sharply, challenges me.

I tighten my grip, teeth bared, breath rough as a growl.

I don't want her.

I can't want her.

I repeat it like a mantra.

Another yank, another step forward. My boots dig into the dirt. Sweat drips down my back.

I don't know how long it lasts. All I know is that my heart is hammering, my chest rising and falling in ragged breaths, my body wound tight to the breaking point.

And then, I feel it.

The moment he surrenders.

The moment all the tension, all the resistance, fades away.

The horse lowers his head, exhales softly.

I shut my eyes, clenching my jaw.

Enough.

She's not mine.

She can't be mine.

I release my grip and take a deep breath.

I force myself back into control.

Then I head back to the stables, my body drained, my nerves still taut.

And as I put away the lead and drag a hand through my sweat-damp hair, I know—no matter how many times I try to fight this—she's still there.

In my head.

In my body.

Everywhere I fucking look.

And God help me, because I don't know how much longer I can hold myself back.

I can't afford to remember the way her breath hitched under my gaze, the way her pupils dilated, the way her body responded to mine... without me even touching her.

Chapter 9

Paola

New day, new training, same asshole.
I repeat it like a mantra, stomping toward my cabin.
I slam the door so hard the walls shudder. My heart hammers. I won't set foot on his side of the ranch for the rest of the day. Hell, for the rest of my life, if possible.
No accidental run-ins. No stolen glances that make me want to slap him. Or worse—kiss him. Or worse—shove him against a wall.
And as sure as death, what happened the other night will never happen again.
It all started with the intention of putting him in his place, of teaching him a lesson because I refused to accept the idea of having him as my trainer.
And instead?
Boom.
Just like that, I fell for it. Again.

Forty-five minutes later, and one long, scalding shower after, I'm ready.
Clean. Relaxed.

And, unfortunately, satisfied. But not enough.

With a sigh, I slip into a yellow sundress, the light fabric brushing against my thighs in a way that feels unfamiliar. Different from my usual dusty jeans. Different from me.

New. Determined. Unshakable.

That's the plan, anyway. Because tonight, I have one clear goal: throw myself into cooking, make my signature potato salad, and pretend Marco Riva doesn't exist.

End of story.

When I step into the kitchen of the main house, I find my mother already at the stove. My father is nowhere to be seen, but the table is set. I raise an eyebrow when I notice four place settings.

"Are we expecting guests?" I ask, glancing at my mother as she smiles at me over whatever's bubbling in the pot. Judging by the smell, it's her signature beef stew.

My mouth is already watering as I get to work peeling the potatoes.

"You didn't think we'd let that poor boy eat alone all the time, did you?" she says, grabbing an extra spoon to taste the sauce.

Please tell me this isn't happening.

But I know damn well it is.

My parents have always had a ridiculous soft spot for Marco.

I grip the knife tighter, taking it out on an innocent potato. Poor thing never saw it coming. "Who exactly are you talking about?" I ask, pretending I don't follow her train of thought.

But my mother isn't an idiot.

She gives me a look that says *nice try*, but answers anyway.

"He's been holed up in that guesthouse, barely coming around... says he doesn't want to intrude," she explains, her expression softening in a way I do *not* appreciate.

Oh, I know exactly what he's been doing in that guesthouse.

Not so different from what you were doing in the shower just now, my annoying inner voice chimes in.

"But your father and I want to make sure he knows he's family here. That he's welcome."

Like hell he is.

I stab the knife into the potato with maybe a little too much force.

Marco Riva is everywhere. In my head. In my damn shower.

And now, at my family dinner table, too.

Straight from the pages of Paola Lux's personal book of disasters.

Chapter 10

Marco

The sun is setting behind the hills as Antonio and I cross the yard, beers in hand, talking about the next competition.

"Elm Hollow is a tricky course," Antonio says, shaking his head. "The footing is unpredictable, and the turn after the second jump has taken down more horses than I care to count."

I nod. "Luna's got talent, but if we don't train her to handle that turn, we can forget about the podium."

Antonio sips his beer. "She needs to work her legs before the break. Keep the pressure on without wearing her out."

I grin. "Exactly. We could simulate that turn in our training course. Get her into the right rhythm before the event."

Antonio gives me a satisfied look. "You've got the right mind for this job, kid."

I'm about to reply when we step into the main house—and that's when I see her.

Paola.

Shit.

Wild hair, loose strands framing her face. Sun-kissed skin. And that damn yellow sundress clinging to all the right places, light enough to hint at the curve of her hips, her legs... Jesus. My throat goes dry.

A simple tie at the waist—one pull, and it would be gone.

Fuck.

I'm talking to her father. Sitting at her family's table. Taking advantage of their kindness. I'm a goddamn bastard.

I try to curse myself out in every way I know how... but my brain and my body are both locked on Paola.

She looks up, as if sensing my thoughts, and sees me. For a moment—a brief, intense moment—she freezes too. Then, just like that, she's composed. Glaring at me like I'm dirt under her boot. A nuisance. At best, a problem to be handled.

Perfect.

Silvia beams, blissfully unaware of the wildfire inside me. "Marco, sit down, dear! We're happy to have you."

"I don't know how to thank you." I clear my throat, embarrassed. If they had any idea what was running through my head right now... they'd throw me out in disgust.

I set down my beer and muster my best smile. I have real affection for Antonio and Silvia, so it doesn't take much effort... even if I feel like absolute shit for having these thoughts about their only daughter.

Antonio sits. I go to follow—then realize the horror of my situation.

The only open seat is right across from her.

Fantastic.

I lower myself into the chair and meet Paola's gaze. Deep, piercing blue eyes, sharp with frustration. Or anger. Maybe both. Wouldn't be the first time.

I settle in. This dinner might get interesting. As much as I hate to admit it, I've always loved sparring with her.

As Silvia serves the stew, Paola places a large bowl of potato salad in the center of the table. I only now realize how hungry I am, and after the first bite, I can't hold back.

"Damn, this is amazing," I say, looking at Silvia. "Absolutely perfect."

Paola freezes mid-slice as she cuts the bread. Then, slowly, she raises an eyebrow.

Silvia laughs. "Oh, thank you, but it's not mine. Paola made it."

My fork stops halfway to my mouth.

Shit.

I look at Paola. She looks at me.

Her smile is sharp as a knife. "Surprised, Riva?"

"A little." I tilt my head, pretending to study her. "I thought your greatest talents were telling me to go to hell and getting dust all over your ass."

Silvia gasps and gives me an affectionate smack on the arm.

Antonio chuckles, shaking his head. "Son, you planning to make it out of here alive?"

Paola clenches her jaw, but there's a spark in her eyes—a challenge that sends heat rushing to places it has no business going at a family dinner.

"Eat your salad, cowboy."

Her voice is sweet as honey. The unspoken message? Shut up, or I'll stab you with my fork.

I smirk and take another bite, this time holding her gaze as I chew slowly.

"Delicious."

Paola flushes—just slightly—then attacks the bread like it personally offended her.

But my mind is a hellhole, because soon enough, I'm wondering just how long that damn dress would last on her before someone—me—took it off.

Dinner continues with easy conversation and talk about the ranch, but every so often, Paola and I exchange jabs like gunslingers waiting to draw.

She gives me that superior look that makes me want to... Well, best not to think about that right now.

"So, Marco," Silvia says as Paola idly spins her fork between her fingers. "How does it feel to be on the other side of the fence? I mean, training instead of competing?"

She asks with that motherly warmth she always has, whether talking to me or her daughter.

"Satisfying," I answer, taking a sip of beer. "I like seeing my students progress. Even the stubborn ones." I throw a not-so-subtle look at my favorite stubborn pain in the ass.

She arches a brow, not missing the jab. "Stubborn? Oh, you mean the ones who actually have a brain and don't fall for your cowboy charm?"

Antonio laughs, but Silvia gives her a warning glance. "Paola, don't be rude."

"I'm just curious, Mom." She smiles at me, fake as my attempt to act unaffected. "I'm sure Marco is very skilled at getting his students to do exactly what he wants."

I hold her gaze, amused. "Let's just say I know how to persuade someone when necessary. Even those who pretend they don't want to listen."

She leans forward slightly, resting her elbows on the table.

Holy hell.

The only thing I can focus on now is the view down her neckline.

"Persuade or manipulate?"

Manipulate? Ah, so we're playing dirty now.

Silvia sighs. "Paola..."

I, on the other hand, just smirk, tilting my head. "You know damn well that if I wanted to manipulate someone, I'd use much more... persuasive methods."

Paola's jaw tightens, but the flush on her cheeks tells me she caught the double meaning.

Antonio watches us closely, then clears his throat. "It'd be nice to see you two work together without fighting every three seconds."

"Oh, but we work just fine together," I say with a grin. "Right, Dusty?"

Paola shoots me a sharp look. "Of course we do."

I shake my head, laughing.

She smiles sweetly, but her eyes say *in your wildest dreams, cowboy*.

Silvia sighs, exchanging a look with Antonio. "Antonio, do you remember when our Paola was sweet and well-mannered?"

Antonio chuckles. "Never seen that version."

Paola lets out an exaggerated sigh and turns her attention back to her food.

Then—bam—a sharp kick under the table.

I jerk forward slightly, biting back a grin, while she casually helps herself to more stew with the most innocent expression in the world.

Lord help me, this woman is going to drive me insane.

And she knows it damn well.

Chapter 11

Marco

Hard work didn't do a damn thing.

Again.

I swore I'd keep myself in check... but the second I stepped into the dependance, I got myself off *again*, thinking about her. About the way she shakes those damn short, wild curls. That dirty mouth. It's been weeks, and I'm still stuck in this damn cycle.

It hasn't passed. I can't get her out of my head.

The moment I walk into the Hollow Saloon, heads turn.

Elm Hollow is a small town. Everybody knows everybody. But I don't know a damn soul in this backwater anymore. I've been gone for ten years. And even back then... I wasn't exactly on track to be town mayor. Spent all my time at the Lux Ranch. Always with the horses. Sometimes with Mr. Lux.

The only real friend I got is Rob... and he's a whole world away. In Los Angeles. Wouldn't mind talking to him right about now. But tonight? I'll settle for alcohol. Nothing else has cleared my head.

I plant myself at the bar and order.

I don't have a clue who the hell the bartender is. And this hole-in-the-wall isn't anything special. But it's the only place around.

I knock back my first drink in one go, grimacing. *Christ, that's awful.*

But I still order another. Because I need it.

And then I hear it.

A laugh.

Her laugh.

Low, rough, real.

It slams into my gut like a red-hot blade.

I turn.

And there she is.

Sitting at a table, beer in hand, smiling wide, eyes bright. She's talking to some girl, but it's the *other* person at the table who makes my blood run cold.

Blond. Wiry. About her age. His arm is slung over her shoulder, fingers brushing against the bare skin at the curve of her neck. She doesn't move away.

No.

She laughs again, tilting her head toward him. Letting him touch her.

Something detonates in my chest.

She's soft with him. Light. There's no tension like when she's with me, no fire that eats her alive every time she looks at me. With him, there's nothing to fight. She's relaxed. Carefree.

And I want to set the whole damn place on fire.

I'm about two seconds from getting up and ripping his goddamn arm off because she's—

She's not yours.

She can't be yours.

I grit my teeth until my jaw aches.

"Just give me the damn bottle and keep the change," I mutter to the bartender before he can pour my next drink.

Then I walk out, whiskey in hand, putting as much distance between me and that table as possible—before I change my mind and break that pretty boy in half.

Because he looks like he fits right next to her. And the only thing I'd ever bring her is trouble.

Chapter 12

Paola

I laugh.

Maybe a little too loud, but who the hell cares?

Maria's telling some crazy story about her sister, Tina, and I can't help but double over, clutching my stomach. Even Matteo laughs beside me, shaking his head. I lean into him, resting my forehead on his shoulder for support.

Just the three of us, tucked in a corner, away from the too-loud music and the crush at the bar.

It's a quiet night—or at least it should be. I'm trying to distract myself.

Then I feel it.

A shiver, sharp and sudden.

No. No way.

I stiffen before I can stop myself, my fingers tightening around my glass. My heart kicks up, some deep, instinctual pull making me turn—right in time to see *him*.

Marco.

Standing near the bar. A bottle clenched in that damn big hand. His dark eyes locked on me. And just like that, my blood turns to ice.

A blink. A breath. But it's enough.

I see it all. I *feel* it all.

The clenched jaw. The heavy breaths. The fire smoldering in his eyes. The raw, burning anger.

And then—like I'm nothing—he turns and walks out.

No words. No expression. No effort to hide just how much he fucking despises me.

He despises me.

My chest tightens. A knot rises in my throat, cutting off my breath.

What the hell. What *the hell*.

Did he have a good laugh when I walked into his damn guesthouse?

Get over it, Paola. Move on.

He keeps treating me like I'm some pathetic little girl, like I'm—wrong.

Humiliation crashes over me like a tidal wave, thick and sickening.

And then comes the rage.

Hot. Fast. Venomous.

Fuck *him*.

Fuck that look, fuck the way he makes me feel.

He can stare at me all damn morning, ordering me to grip the saddle tighter in that low, dirty voice of his—but then he turns around and acts like I'm a *mistake?*

No.

Hell no.

For a second, I actually thought he wanted me.

That he was fighting it because I'm his boss's daughter.

But no—he's just the same asshole I always knew he was.

He's playing games.

I grab the tequila, pour a shot, fill the glass to the brim.

"Paola, you sure about that?" Maria asks, watching me closely.

No.
But what does it matter?
I lift the glass and knock it back in one go.
It burns—like Marco's fucking stare. Like the knot strangling me.
But it's not enough.
I take another.
I laugh louder, pressing in closer to Matteo. He looks confused, but I don't care.
If Marco thinks I'm just some spoiled little girl—
Fine.
I'll move on.
At least, that's what I keep telling myself.

Chapter 13

Marco

Fucking Paola.

Fucking sexy laugh.

Fucking blond kid with his arm around her—like he had any damn right.

I curl my fingers around the neck of the bottle as I walk, my jaw clenched, breath coming out in sharp bursts through my nose. My grip tightens until my knuckles ache, every muscle strung tight, forcing me away.

Away from her.

Without thinking, I climb into the pickup and fire up the engine.

I drive. No direction. No destination.

Elm Hollow's streets are empty, barely lit by rusted-out streetlamps. Radio stays off. I don't want to hear a damn thing. The town sign vanishes in the rearview. I hit the highway, then veer onto a dirt road going nowhere.

Ten minutes later, I kill the engine.

Silence.

I get out, lean against the pickup, crack open the bottle. First sip burns like hell. Second one's worse.

But it's not enough.

Doesn't erase a damn thing.

It doesn't erase the way I *feel* about her.

Doesn't erase how bad I wanted to rip that damn dress off.

It doesn't erase the way I wanted to take her when she whispered, *What if I stayed?*

I drag a hand down my face, then sink to the ground, back against the truck's wheel.

Fucking mistake.

Fucking idiot.

I lift the bottle to my lips—

Then stop.

Clench my teeth.

Enough.

I'm not the man I thought I was. Not decent. Not honorable. Hell, not even close.

Because fuck no, I'm not letting another man have her.

Paola Lux is mine.

Paola Lux is mine. And I'm about to make that crystal. Fucking. Clear.

Chapter 14

Paola

The night air bites at my skin as I stumble out of the bar, tequila heat burning slow and steady through my veins—liquid anesthesia.

It's loosened my muscles, given me the courage to laugh louder, throw bolder glances. Forget—for a few blissful moments. That look.

His look.

Fuck. Why won't he stop haunting me?

I see it still—branded into my brain like a red-hot iron.

Marco, watching me before he walked out. Ice in his eyes. Silent, fucking judgment.

Like I was nothing.

Like some stupid little girl playing dress-up.

My fingers curl into fists as I walk down the dirt road, leaning into Matteo for balance. Swallowing the lump clawing up my throat.

What the hell is his problem?

First, he provokes me. He tempts me. He makes me believe there's... something. *Something* between us.

And then he looks at me like that? Like I'm beneath him?

I huff out a sharp breath, shaking my head.

I don't care.

I *can't* care.

Except—
I do.
Too much.
A bitter laugh scrapes up my throat. "You're a fucking idiot, Paola," I mutter under my breath, feeling heat bloom across my cheeks.
Because yeah—
I drank too much.
Yeah, I laughed too loud.
Yeah, I let arms wrap around me that I didn't want, that meant *nothing*.
But none of it was for me.
It was for *him*.
To punish him.
And the worst part?
It didn't do a damn thing.
I'm still here, with my head full of him. Of his hands. Of that dark stare. Of that fucking gravel-rough voice that's been winding around my insides for weeks.
Matteo opens the car door, ready to take me home. Thank God one of us stayed sober. Maria's already gone.
I'm about to climb inside—
When it happens.
A shiver rakes down my spine.
I don't know how—
I just *know*.
He's close.
I feel it before I even turn around.
The air changes—
Thicker. Heavier.
Like the whole night is holding its breath.

And then I see him.

A shadow leaning against his pickup.

Arms crossed over his chest. Face hidden in the dark. Eyes locked *right* on me.

My heart slams so hard against my ribs, I swear it echoes through the whole fucking valley.

He moves.

Slow. Steady.

Coming closer.

My breath snags in my throat.

A tangled mess of fear, anger, and something else.

Something hotter. Deeper.

My body coils tight.

Like it doesn't know whether to run away.

Or run straight into him.

Chapter 15

Marco

Paola smells like tequila and trouble.

She's leaning against that little blond fuck like it's the most natural thing in the world, like she belongs to him. Like she's his.

And it's driving me insane.

Every part of me screams to rip her away from him. Remind her who she was flirting with just hours ago. Make her understand she can't play with me, then let someone else touch her like it's nothing.

But that's the whole fucking point, isn't it? To her, it *is* nothing.

I'm the one who's jerked off to thoughts of her more times than I can count. The one who's worked his ass off just to stop thinking. The one drowning in shitty whiskey, trying to kill the want. The one burning alive from the inside out.

And she's over there, laughing. Letting him hold her like I don't exist.

I move before I think.

My legs close the distance in seconds. Her laughter dies on her lips. Blue eyes widen as she looks up at me.

Not laughing now, are you, Dusty?

The guy stiffens beside her, shifting just a little—but not enough. He's still too close.

Paola steps away from him—slow, hesitant. Which just pisses me off more.

"You're a damn good actress, Dusty." My voice is low, rough. I don't even know from what—the whiskey, the anger, or the ridiculous fucking urge to pin her to the nearest surface.

She tenses. Her eyes narrow, liquid fire cutting right through me.

"What the fuck do you want, *kickass*?" Her voice drips venom, but beneath it, there's something else.

Something I recognize.

Something that makes me smirk.

"I wanna know if it worked."

"If *what* worked?" she spits, jaw tight.

"This." I jerk my chin toward the guy, the tequila, the whole damn circus she's putting on tonight. "This little show."

She scoffs, shaking her head. "Go to hell."

"I'm already there, *Dusty*." *And you're the fucking fire.*

I take another step closer. Now we're too close. She smells of alcohol and stubbornness, and I don't know what the hell I want to do—kiss her or yell at her.

Own her or let her go.

I grab her wrist. Not hard, not enough to hurt. But enough to remind her who the fuck I am.

Enough to remind her who *we* are.

She sucks in a breath. "Let me go."

I don't.

I tighten my grip, just a little. "Tell me you want me to leave."

Silence.

One breath.

One blink.

And then—

"Fuck you, fucking *kickass*."

I smirk. Same filthy mouth.

Paola's breathing is shallow, uneven. Her eyes are locked on mine, blue flames of rage and something else. Something she won't say out loud, but I see it anyway.

And she dares me.

Like she doesn't know who the hell she's playing with.

I tighten my grip on her wrist, step forward, forcing her back until her spine meets the car door. Blondie shifts beside us like he's thinking about stepping in.

One look stops him cold.

"I'd take a step back, *pretty boy*," I say, voice low, calm. But there's nothing reassuring about it. "Unless you want me to explain the hard way why you don't touch what isn't yours."

Blondie prince raises a brow and steps forward anyway. The little shit's got guts. I'll give him that.

"What the hell are you talking about?" he asks, looking at me like I'm crazy. "She's my cousin."

I don't care.

I don't care *who* the fuck he is to her.

I don't care that I have no right to do this.

I only care that I can't fucking take it anymore.

And I can't hold back.

I drop my gaze to Paola. She's still trapped between me and the car, chest rising and falling too fast, fists clenched at her sides.

She's waiting for me to let go.

Waiting for me to back off.

Waiting for me to do the right thing.

Fuck the right thing.

My hand leaves her wrist, slides to her waist.

And then she's over my shoulder.

Paola yelps, kicking, struggling, fists hammering against my back. "*Marco! Put me down!*"

"Not a chance, *Dusty*." My voice is a low growl.

"Are you out of your fucking mind?!" She keeps fighting, her fists like a damn kitten's claws, scratching at me like they could do any real damage.

I glance back at Blondie. He's frozen, eyes wide.

"Relax, champ." I give him a sharp grin. "The big bad wolf's not gonna eat her. Even if he came for her."

Then I turn and walk away, my wild little Dusty thrashing in my arms.

And I don't stop until we're alone.

Until she's in my pickup.

I fire up the engine and we're gone.

Chapter 16

Marco

The pickup hums under the dim streetlights. The engine rumbles, low and steady, blending with the pounding in my chest. I press the accelerator, trying to pull myself together.

Paola sits rigid in the passenger seat, jaw clenched, chest rising too fast. She's pissed. Pissed as hell. But beneath it, there's something else. I see it in the way her thighs press together, in the way she wets her lips without even realizing it.

The silence stretches, a taut rope ready to snap.

I grip the wheel tighter, knuckles white.

Don't look at her. Don't touch her. Don't fuck this up. You've already gone too far.

But I feel her. Fuck, I feel her too much.

The scent of her skin, the heat of her body just inches from mine. The soft sound of her breath.

"You're out of your mind, you know that?" Her voice is low, sharp.

I don't answer. I keep my eyes fixed on the road ahead.

Paola laughs, a low, venomous sound. "What, now you're not talking? You get off on dragging me away like I'm your damn property, and then you ignore me?" She leans in. "Did you think I'd be scared? That I'd start crying?"

I close my eyes for a brief second. She's playing with fire.

"Say something, for fuck's sake." Her voice rises.

She has no idea about the storm inside me right now. The hell that's been burning through me for weeks.

I slow down, pull over, kill the engine.

I look at her. Really look at her. And the way she stares back—stormy, locked onto mine—wrecks me.

My hand shoots out, grabbing the back of her neck. A quick, hungry move. No control.

Her breath catches, lips parting.

"You want me to say something, Dusty?" My voice is low, hoarse, almost a growl. I lean in, brushing my lips against hers without kissing her. Her scent floods my senses. "Fine. Then hear this—I'm barely holding myself back."

She bites her lip. Christ.

"And what if I don't want you to?" she whispers.

My thumb skims her jaw, drags down her neck. I feel the rapid pulse beneath my fingers. I could kiss her right now. I could wipe that cocky little smirk off her face and show her that this isn't a game.

She swallows. Doesn't pull away. If anything, she leans in closer. Her knee brushes my thigh, her hand resting lightly on mine, as if daring me to move it lower.

Paola Lux is provoking me. Again.

And I'm a fucking idiot.

My hand tightens around her throat—not hard, not enough to hurt, just enough to let her know I've lost control.

"You have no idea what kind of trouble you're getting yourself into, Dusty."

She tilts her chin up, that maddening little smirk still there. "And what if that's exactly what I want?"

A second later, my mouth crashes against hers.

I kiss her with all the anger, frustration, and desire that's been consuming me for weeks. It's desperate, fierce, filled with bites and ragged breaths. My fingers tangle in her hair as I pull her closer, swallowing her moan against my lips.

Her hands grip my shirt, tugging me toward her, her nails scratching my skin beneath the fabric.

Christ, Paola.

Then—just when I'm about to lose myself, just when I'm about to finally touch her—she pulls away.

Her chest rises and falls rapidly, her blue eyes dark and blown wide. Her lips are swollen, red. Her breath is a goddamn invitation to destroy her.

But she leans back, pressing against the seat.

She watches me. Dares me.

And then she smiles. "That's it?"

A low growl rumbles in my chest.

I drag a hand over my jaw, trying to steady my breathing. Then, without warning, I lean in, pressing my body against hers, making sure she feels every inch of what she's doing to me. Making sure she understands that if she wants to play, I'll be the one to make her lose.

I brush my lips against her ear. "Dusty, I swear to God... the next time you push me like this, I'll fuck you right here."

She shivers. I feel it.

She tilts her head back and laughs. And I know I'm fucked.
Because this war... she just won it.

Chapter 17

Paola

The car jerks to a stop, tires screeching against warm asphalt. The engine dies. The only sound left is our pounding hearts. I stare into the darkness, my mind spinning with need.

He steps out first, silent. Then, he turns, eyes locking onto mine. His gaze is locked on me—predatory, intense. Like I'm the only thing that exists. My fingers fumble with the seatbelt, struggling for a second, and when I finally unbuckle it, I waste no time. I step out immediately.

His hands are on me before I can think, rough, urgent. He lifts me off the ground, carrying me toward his dependance. The door slams shut behind us, and then I'm pinned against it. His presence consumes me. Owns me. The darkness is absolute, but nothing has ever been clearer. His body is the only thing I feel, the only thing I want. His hands are fire. Possessive.

He yanks me against him, kisses me like a starved man, then shoves me back against the wall. His breath is fire against my neck. He's strong, rough, and I don't want anything else. His hand slides up my thigh, grips tight, hooks it around his hip. His palm drags up, finds my ass, squeezes hard. The fire inside me burns hotter, and there is nothing I crave more than him. Right now.

Nothing else matters. Nothing ever did.

Our age gap? Nothing. The fact that he's my coach? Who cares? The town whispers? Let them. All that matters is this. Him. Now.

"Dusty…" His voice is low, a whisper against my skin. But I get the sinking feeling he's about to say this is a mistake.

I don't let him.

I kiss him. Desperate. Teeth, tongue, a war neither of us wants to win.

I roll my hips against him, needing to feel him. He's hard. Ready. And fucking huge. I haven't been able to get the image of him stroking himself out of my head since I saw it. I press closer, letting him claim every inch of space between us. His mouth hovers near mine, but he doesn't kiss me— not yet. He waits, studying me, teasing me.

My skin is on fire, and I know I can't take much more.

"You should stop me," he rasps.

I look at him, my heart slamming against my ribs, and answer without hesitation. "Not a chance."

His grin is wicked. Dangerous. And I want him— more than air.

Before I can say another word, his mouth crashes onto mine.

The kiss is a storm. Wild. Relentless. Out of control. His hands roam my body like he's mapping out every inch, and I pull him closer, needing more. Clothes vanish, tossed somewhere neither of us gives a damn about. He looks at me, swallows hard, then cups my breast, his touch rough and reverent at the same time.

I ache for him.

His hands grow bolder, claiming, lifting me effortlessly. I don't resist. I never would. He spins me, pressing me against the wall, his arms caging me in.

I grind against him, my body begging for his. Every breath, every movement is pure need.

"I want you to take me," I whisper against his lips.

He stares at me, his face shadowed by the dim light, his expression unreadable. But I don't care what he's thinking. I only care that he acts.

Then he stops. Just for a second. Like he's hesitating.

No. No, no, no.

I kiss him again, desperate for him to understand how badly I need this.

"Dusty..." His breath is ragged. "Stop."

I pull back, frustration burning in my veins. "What?" My voice is sharp, harsher than I intended. He sees the tension in my face.

He cups my cheek, his touch softer now, his eyes unreadable. I don't think he's ever looked at me like this before.

"I just..." He exhales. "Maybe we should slow down."

What?

Seriously?

He doesn't want me. It's obvious. This was just a moment. And I'm a fool.

"Dusty..." His voice is softer, like he can hear the thoughts racing through my head. "Look at me."

I do. Even though my chest aches, even though I want to disappear.

"I want you more than anything," he says, his voice raw. "But I don't want you just for tonight. I —I can't do this if that's all it is."

And then, in his eyes, I see something I've never seen before. Vulnerability.

"You've been drinking," he adds. "And I need to know that if you decide to be with me, you're in your right mind when you do."

Oh, hell no.

"You absolute idiot," I breathe. "I have never been this fucking sober."

He bursts out laughing. "That mouth."

And then he kisses me again. Slower. Deeper. This time, we savor it. No words. Just us—losing ourselves completely.

Chapter 18

Paola

It's the most beautiful kiss I've ever had. But I'm the one who breaks it.

"I want you to take me," I whisper again, breathless.

I see him struggle. I see it in the way his chest rises and falls, in the way his fingers grip me tighter, as if he's trying to hold back. But I don't want him to hold back.

"Kic-kass," I taunt. I provoke him. I rub against him, his erection pressing between my thighs. "If you don't give me what I want, I'll find someone who will." I taunt. But with anyone else, it wouldn't be the same. I want him. Here, now, forever.

My words hit him like a spark. Anger. Jealousy. Possession.

I watch him break. A deep sound rumbles from his throat.

Then, no more control.

No more fear.

Only him.

Only us.

He presses against me. Hard. Ready.

"I want you inside me," I pant. "I'm on the pill."

He growls, locking eyes with mine. "There are condoms in the other room, if you're not sure" He pauses. "I'm clean."

I shake my head. "I just want you. I want to feel you."

His gaze flickers, pure instinct. Then he devours me.

His fingers tangle in my hair, tilting my head back. His mouth glides over my neck—soft and cruel. He marks me.

He lifts me, my legs wrapping around his waist. He pins me against the wall. Hands everywhere. Skin everywhere. Nothing left between us.

Hot. Fevered. Desperate.

He traps my wrists. Binds me in place.

"Well then..." A smirk. Eyes dark, dangerous. He grabs something from the nearby dresser. "Guess I'll have to tame you."

Reins. Oh, hell.

This man is my undoing.

He ties me up tight. Then he lifts my thigh and slams into me, one rough motion.

I push against him. I want him deeper. Harder.

He obeys.

And he does it without mercy.

He drives into me—brutal, stretching, splitting me open. A cry rips from my lips, but he swallows it with his mouth. He devours me.

The wall scrapes my back. He pounds into me—hard, deep, wild. He is everything I want.

"Look at you." His voice is a growl, low and rough, thick with pleasure. "You were made for me."

The tight knot of leather holding me bound strains as I try to move my hands. I am his. I can't do anything but take him, feel him, let him consume me.

"Tell me you want it."

"I want it."

"Tell me who you belong to."

Heat explodes inside me. I slam against him, my hips desperate, chasing, needing. There's no stopping now.

He slams into me harder, his grip on my thighs turning bruising. He crashes into me, the sound of skin against skin filling the room. Obscene. Animalistic.

I moan. He growls.

His hands close around my throat. Steady. Not to hurt—just to feel my voice vibrate against his skin.

He feels me tighten around him. Feels my body surrender.

I explode. I scream his name.

He follows right after, his mouth on my skin, his breath ragged, his pleasure breaking inside me.

And then silence.

Breathless. Tangled. Our hearts hammering. Me inside him. Him inside me.

He unties me, fingers tracing the marks the reins left behind. Then he pulls me in. Tight. Like he'll never let go.

I don't know how long we stay like this. Only that I never want it to end.

Chapter 19

Marco

Soft, rosy light filters through the curtains. The day is slowly breaking, and I wake up with Paola's warm body molded against mine.

I breathe her in—the scent of her, mixed with sex and the sweat of the night. My hand is still on her bare skin, her back pressed to my chest, her breath slow and steady.

It's surreal. It's perfect.

And for a long moment, I don't think about anything.

I trace my fingers along her side, drawing lazy circles on her soft skin. She stirs just slightly, a low hum slipping from her lips, but she doesn't wake.

I tighten my arm around her and bury my face in her hair.

And right in that moment, reality slams into me like a punch to the chest.

What the hell have I done?

She shifts a little, turning toward me. Her eyes are still half-closed, her lips a little swollen, her hair a mess—beautiful.

She looks at me and then smiles.

And I'm fucked.

"Morning, Kickass." Her voice is husky with sleep.

My stomach clenches. I have no idea what to say.

She stretches, the sheet sliding over her body, slipping low enough to reveal her bare breasts. My gaze drags over her before I can stop it. God, I had her—every inch of her—and I want her all over again.

And yet... there's a part of me already falling apart.

Because last night wasn't just a fuck.

Not with her.

And that's exactly the problem.

She notices my silence. Studies me. The smile fades just a little. "You're already overthinking, aren't you?"

I drop my gaze, sighing. "Paola..."

"Don't," she cuts me off instantly. She props herself up on one elbow. "Don't ruin this."

I shake my head, staring at the ceiling, trying to find a way to say what's clawing at my chest.

"I... I don't want to ruin your life." My voice is low, almost tired. "If people find out..."

"I don't give a fuck about people."

Her answer is immediate. Sharp. It hits me square in the chest.

She moves closer, cups my face in both hands, forcing me to look at her.

"Do you want this?" she asks, and her eyes cut straight through me.

I swallow. Fuck. "Of course I do."

She leans in even more. "Then what's the problem?"

I shake my head, frustrated. "I'm too old for you."

She scoffs. "Oh, here we go. The bullshit argument."

"Paola, I'm ten years older than you."

She lifts a brow. "And?"

"And... you have your whole life ahead of you."

She stares at me for a second, then laughs—a low, almost incredulous sound.

"And you don't?" she asks, a crooked smile tugging at her lips. "What are you, Marco? Some old, washed-up man?"

I roll my eyes. "That's not the point."

She climbs on top of me, hands planted on my chest. "The point is, you're looking for an excuse to run."

I open my mouth to argue, but she shuts me up by kissing me. Slow. Deep. Unhurried.

When she pulls back, her eyes lock onto mine.

"I want you. Period."

My throat tightens. My heart pounds hard.

"If you want to leave, then go," she says. "But don't do it because you think you know what's best for me."

I stare at her.

God, this girl is going to destroy me.

And the worst part?

I don't want to run.

I want to stay.

I want her.

And that terrifies me more than anything.

Chapter 20

Marco

Paola's still in my bed when I decide.

If we're doing this, we're doing it for real.

I don't want to be a secret. I don't want to be something she hides or a story she forgets when things get complicated.

I want her. Really want her.

And if I do, I have to face her father.

I run a hand down my face and take a slow breath. Fuck.

Paola watches me from the bed.

God... I want to see her like this forever.

In my bed, satisfied, smiling.

She's beautiful, but more than that, she's stubborn.

She already knows.

I climb back into bed, not wanting to waste a second away from her.

"I know what you're thinking," she says, that mix of teasing and challenge in her voice.

I lift a brow. "Oh yeah?"

She nods. "You want to talk to my father."

I don't even try to deny it.

She sighs. "Marco, you know you don't have to."

"No," I cut her off. "I do."

She bites her lip, the first sign of nerves I've seen in her since she decided this—*us*—was happening.

I shake my head. "Paola... your father gave me everything."

She sits up, watching me.

"I was an arrogant kid with more trouble than discipline," I say, my voice quieter. "And he held me up when everything else could've come crashing down."

I rake a hand through my hair, searching for the right words.

"He got me a spot on the team. He believed in me when no one else did. And when the racing world got too toxic—when I couldn't take the pressure, the money, the expectations anymore—he was the one who told me to walk away... and he wasn't even disappointed."

Paola listens in silence, eyes locked on mine.

"He told me to go back to the roots, to find a place where I could remember why I loved horses."

I let out a slow, bitter smile. "And he gave me this. A job. A place to live. A second chance."

A long silence stretches between us.

Then I lift my gaze to her.

"And now," I say quietly, "I've gone and fallen in love with his daughter."

Paola doesn't say a word. She just looks at me, her face more open, more vulnerable than usual.

My stomach tightens.

"I can't disrespect him."

She drops her gaze, then nods slowly. "I know."

She doesn't say anything else.

For a second, I worry she's angry.

But then she moves, naked and stunning, straddling my lap.

She cups my face in her hands.

"If you think I don't know how much he means to you, you're wrong," she whispers. "And *because* I know... *because* I know who you are, Marco, I know you don't need his permission to be with me."

I inhale slowly. God.

She leans in, her lips brushing mine. "But if talking to him makes *you* feel better... then do it."

I smile, shaking my head. "Thanks for the permission, Dusty."

She huffs, but she's smiling too.

Then she kisses me.

And for a moment, Antonio disappears completely from my mind.

Paola's hands move over my skin, exploring, claiming. "So, Kick-ass... you're in love with me?"

Her voice is low, husky, downright sinful.

How the hell could I not be?

I don't answer with words. I push her back gently, laying her down on the bed, and just *look* at her, my breath heavy.

My Dusty isn't exactly a sweet, delicate princess. If anything... she's got the filthiest mouth I've ever heard. And I love it.

I kiss my way down her body, savoring every shiver, every sigh.

When I reach her thighs, her fingers tangle in my hair, and the low moan that escapes her makes me lose my damn mind.

"This pretty pussy is mine, you know that, right?" I murmur against her hot skin.

She nods, breathless.

I taste her slowly, deliberately, and the flavor of her hits me like a punch to the chest. Sweet as honey. Intense as *her*.

Her body tightens under my mouth, her sighs turning into deep, desperate moans as I build her up. I take my time, exploring her with my tongue, making her tremble beneath me.

Only when I feel her teetering on the edge do I suck her clit harder, and her back arches, pleasure ripping through her.

I move back up, savoring every second.

Paola looks at me, her chest rising fast, her cheeks flushed, her eyes burning.

I smile, brushing my lips against hers.

"I love you, Dusty."

And this time, I say it. Because it's the truth.

And because I've never wanted anyone the way I want her.

"I love you too, Kick-ass."

Chapter 21

Marco

My hands never sweat. *Never*. Not even when I was about to clear an impossible jump or when I could hear my opponent's breath right behind me, just meters from the finish line.

And yet, here we are.

Palms damp, stomach twisted, guilt heavy on my chest.

Antonio sits on the porch, a steaming cup of coffee in his hands, his gaze fixed on the paddocks. He always looks the same—solid, unshakable, like an oak standing firm in the middle of a storm.

I step closer, clear my throat.

He doesn't turn.

"If you're here to tell me one of the colts escaped again, save me the trouble of getting pissed off."

Perfect. Just the welcome I needed.

I take a deep breath and move closer. "No, no runaway horses today."

I sit beside him, clasp my hands together, and try to find the right words.

He takes a slow sip of coffee, like a man who already knows something's coming. "Spit it out, kid."

I stare at him, a little thrown. "Am I that obvious?"

He snorts. Then laughs. "Son, you look like a dead man walking... Usually, you're a damn clown. So yeah."

Not sure if that's supposed to be a compliment.

Antonio looks at me, then sighs and shakes his head with a half-smile. "You've always been a good kid," he says, like he already knows I'm afraid to tell him.

And those words hit me harder than they should.

How much longer will he think that?

"I..." I swallow. I don't know how to say this.

He just keeps watching me.

"I know I've never repaid you for everything you've done for me... and I've probably been a disappointment more than once..." I start. My heart's about to punch its way out of my chest.

How do you look a man in the eye—the man who's been like a father to you—and drop the one thing that might make him stop believing in you?

"Kid," he says with a half-smile, "you piss me off plenty. But disappoint me? That's a lot harder to do."

Antonio studies me for a long moment. Then he sets down his coffee, stands up, takes a step toward me, and claps a heavy hand on my shoulder.

"You know I already know, right?" His voice is serious.

What? Are we even talking about the same thing?

"I didn't want it to happen," I say quickly. "I mean, I *did*, but not like this. I never wanted to disrespect you."

Antonio sighs. "Marco."

I lift my head, tense.

He studies me, then chuckles and shakes his head. "Kid, if you think telling me you're in love with my daughter is the issue, you're dumber than I thought."

I freeze.

He shoots me a look that says, *You're more predictable than you think, idiot.*

"I'm old, not stupid." He takes another sip of coffee. "It was only a matter of time."

The anxiety inside me eases—a fraction.

"And honestly... you've always been like a son to me. I couldn't have asked for better for my little girl."

I swallow hard. My eyes burn.

The love this man has given me—*still* gives me—overshadows everything.

I pull him into a hug, unable to say a damn word.

"Don't go soft on me now, kid... Takes balls to run this ranch."

I look up, stunned.

"...What?"

"Son, you really think I don't wanna retire?"

He lets out a deep, rumbling laugh.

Then we sit back down, drinking coffee together.

More relaxed.

Or at least, *I'm* more relaxed...

He just had fun making me sweat.

Epilogue

Paola

The air smells of rain-soaked earth and adrenaline.

The crowd is a distant hum, muffled—like the whole world has narrowed to this single moment. Me, Luna, and the final obstacle standing between us and victory.

I tighten the reins, my heart pounding in my chest. She trembles beneath me, muscles coiled like a spring ready to unleash. It's her first competition, her first real test, yet it feels like I've known her forever. I know how she breathes, how she thinks.

And I know she wants to win just as much as I do.

I hear Marco's voice from the sidelines, an encouragement that washes over me like a wave of warmth, even if I can't make out the words.

My coach. My partner. The love of my life.

We take the final turn. The wind lashes my skin, my heartbeat syncing with the rhythmic pound of her hooves on the sand.

Luna surges forward. I can feel her power, her determination.

The last jump is right in front of us.

I hold my breath.

One. Two. Three. We leap.

For a split second, we are weightless—suspended in perfect harmony, two hearts beating as one.

We land as light as a feather.

And then...

The finish line is behind us, and the air erupts with sound.

We won.

My breath catches in my throat. The world rushes back in—the cheers, the applause, the overwhelming euphoria.

I lean forward, threading my fingers through Luna's mane.

"Good girl," I whisper, my voice shaking with emotion. "So damn good."

I stroke her, inhaling deeply. My champion. My star.

But it's not over.

I slide off the saddle, my feet hitting the ground with a weightlessness that doesn't feel real. Then I turn.

And I see him.

Marco is running toward me, his eyes shining, his face lit up with the biggest, most beautiful smile in the world.

I don't even think. I run too.

We crash into each other halfway, his arms wrapping around me, my hands clutching him like he's the only thing keeping me tethered to the earth.

Spoiler: *He is*.

He laughs, holding me tighter. "You're incredible."

I laugh too, my fingers tangling in his hair, my heart hammering so hard it makes my head spin. "I know."

He pulls back just enough to look at me, and in his eyes, I see it all.

Our story. Our future.

The certainty that there is nowhere else in the world I'd rather be.

We are the new owners of Lux Ranch. And next year, he'll be my husband.

"I love you, kick-ass," I whisper against his lips.

He smiles, kissing me like time has stopped.

And maybe, in this moment, it really doesn't.

Thank you for reading *Dusty*! If you loved Paola and Marco's story, you'll definitely fall for their children's adventures.

Start with *Saddle and Bound*—available now on Amazon!

Keep reading for a sneak peek of Saddle and Bound (book 1) and Unmasked (book 2).

Saddle and Bound

Chapter 1

Rosie

"Service announcement: a pair of red panties has been found. The owner can go to the console to retrieve it."

I listen absentmindedly from my lounger under the sun. My groggy brain takes a few seconds to process the announcement. A few more seconds to realize I could be the owner... but you know that annoying sixth sense that tells you something, only for your reason to step in and warn you about your own paranoia? Well, my reason convinces me that I'm just being paranoid.

But still... that nagging feeling refuses to let me relax.

"Rosie, I think these are definitely yours," Lexy announces, just as irritating as my inner voice. As always, she gives voice to her thoughts without thinking.

I open my eyes to find Lexy standing in front of me, holding up a pair of red lace panties, her mischievous grin making my blood rush to my cheeks. I can't quite process the absurdity of the situation. "What are they doing there?" I stammer, trying to maintain some composure.

"I got them from the DJ at the console," Lexy explains, chuckling. "He said they were found on the path leading to the stables. Seems like your style."

I hear a male laugh behind me and turn around abruptly. Alex, the ranch's riding instructor, approaches with an amused expression. "Ah, so that's where it ended up," he says, looking at me with a sly smile. "I found them while checking on the horses and took them to the console."

I feel like I'm about to explode with a mix of embarrassment and anger. "Yes, it's mine," I reply curtly, trying to sound neutral. "Thanks for finding them."

Alex raises an eyebrow, still amused. "Are you sure they're yours?" he asks, holding the panties just out of my reach.

"Alex, stop being childish," Valentina intervenes, trying to suppress a laugh. "Give Rosie her panties."

Finally, Alex hands them to me with a theatrical flourish, and I snatch them from his hand, stuffing them into my bag with as much dignity as I can muster. Lexy keeps laughing, while I do my best to avoid Alex's piercing gaze.

"How funny," I mutter, though my tone is anything but amused.

"You know, Rosie," Alex says, his voice relaxed in that way that drives me crazy, "you could loosen up a little. We're not in Los Angeles here. No one's judging you."

I look at him, biting back the sharp response I'm dying to give. "Thanks for the advice," I reply with a tight smile. "But I think I know how to relax."

Alex grins again, tilting his head slightly. "We'll see," he says simply, before walking away, leaving me with a mix of embarrassment and frustration.

Chapter 2

Rosie

One day before

After nearly 24 hours of travel, with intercontinental flights and multiple layovers, I feel as though I've crossed not just an ocean, but an entire universe. Los Angeles feels like a distant memory as my dad's car winds along the twisting road leading to Sunrise Ranch, nestled on the outskirts of a small town in southern Italy.

My eyes, heavy with jet lag, scan the landscape outside the window: rolling hills, centuries-old olive groves, hay bales, and golden wheat fields stretching as far as the eye can see. It's a world completely different from the skyscrapers and constant traffic I'm used to. Occasionally, my dad's red Fiat passes people on horseback, tractors, and the typical Ape motorcycles on the road.

It feels like I've not only changed world... but also era. Everything seems so absurd and strange...

I absentmindedly run a hand through my hair, trying to tame the red locks that the journey has tousled. I try not to think about how disastrous I must look. The anxiety, which I tried to suppress during the long flight, now returns with force. Three months. Three whole months in this remote village. How will I survive? My job at the marketing agency, my routine, my life... everything put on hold for my father's wedding. Thankfully, I managed to take a little time off from work, using up some vacation days I'd accumulated but never taken, along with a bit of remote work. At least my career is safe, for now.

"We're almost there," Dad announces, his voice betraying a mixture of fatigue and excitement. "Val and Lexy can't wait to finally meet you in person."

I nod, trying to appear casual and happy while struggling to smooth out the wrinkles in my crumpled suit. I suddenly feel out of place dressed like this. I hadn't even considered that my office attire and sky-high heels might make me feel even more self-conscious. Usually, I like to dress well. I like being impeccable and elegant. I don't mind other types of clothing... but I simply never find myself in situations that call for more casual attire. What I do dislike is feeling sticky, not having perfectly styled hair, and not having flawless makeup.

"How much longer?" I ask, my voice hoarse from fatigue.

"Just about ten minutes," Dad replies. "You'll see, the ranch is beautiful. You'll like it."

I sigh, resting my head against the window. The humid heat of southern Italy seeps into the car despite the air conditioning, making me long for California's dry climate.

When the car finally stops in front of an imposing gate with the words **SUNRISE RANCH**, I realize we've arrived.

We pass through the impressive wrought-iron gate, and as the car proceeds along the driveway lined with towering pines and firs, I can't help but look around, trying to absorb every detail. The trees flanking the entrance open up, revealing a breathtaking landscape that leaves me speechless.

To our right, a vast olive grove extends as far as the eye can see, the silver leaves of the olive trees dancing in the light breeze. To the left, I glimpse a lush orchard, branches laden with ripe peaches and golden apricots. The air is infused with their sweet scent, mixed with the pungent aroma of wild rosemary.

Further ahead, I spot an enclosure where several horses graze peacefully. Their sleek coats shine under the sun, and the sound of their occasional neighs breaks the silence of the countryside.

As the car advances, I notice several wooden cabins scattered across the property. Some are hidden among holm oak groves, others overlook small, thriving vegetable gardens.

Each structure seems to have its own unique character, inviting exploration.

In the distance, a field of hay bales creates a golden expanse stretching to the horizon. Spots of vivid red dot the field on the sides—wild poppies, I imagine—adding splashes of color to the landscape.

As we approach the end of the driveway, I finally see it: the main house. It's a limestone farmhouse, imposing yet welcoming, with olive-green shutters and a red-tiled roof. A veranda shaded by a pergola of flowering wisteria extends along the facade, promising a cool retreat from hot summer days.

The car stops in front of the house, and for a moment, I remain motionless, overwhelmed by the beauty surrounding me. Sunrise Ranch is more than I could have ever imagined: a corner of paradise that leaves me speechless. At this moment, overwhelmed by everything around me, I forget all that was bothering and annoying me earlier.

A group of young people is waiting for us in the garden. Two girls run toward us.

"Robert! Rosie! You're finally here!"

The shorter of the two is a bundle of energy, with long, wavy light brown hair and bright hazel eyes. The other is her exact opposite: tall and with a rebellious air accentuated by piercings and tattoos.

I get out of the car, stumbling on my heels. "Nice to meet you," I say, trying to smile despite my nervousness.

"We're so happy you're here!" exclaims the one with long, wavy hair—she must be Valentina. I'm immediately swept into a hug and receive two kisses on the cheeks. The other girl does the same, but with less energy. Lexy… if I remember correctly.

"How was the trip?" someone asks.

I'm about to answer when a male voice makes me turn abruptly.

"Hey, princess, careful not to break an ankle!"

I find myself standing face-to-face with a man who looks like he's walked straight out of a forbidden fantasy.

He's tall, broad-shouldered, and muscular, with long brown hair that falls in unruly waves, framing a face almost too handsome to belong to reality. That crooked smile he's wearing, equal parts maddening and devastatingly sexy, hits me like a bolt of lightning.

His deep brown eyes, sharp and unashamedly confident, are framed by lashes so thick they might as well be illegal. A light dusting of scruff shadows his strong jawline, adding a rugged edge to a face that's already doing far too much damage to my self-control.

He's dressed in a snug, well-worn tank top that clings to every ridge of his sculpted torso, leaving absolutely nothing to the imagination. His broad chest commands attention, and the way his body narrows to a lean, powerful waist is downright scandalous. Paired with faded, low-slung jeans and mud-caked boots, he exudes an effortless, rugged charm that feels both untamed and dangerously attractive.

Pull yourself together, Rosie, I scold myself fiercely.

I fight to look away, but the heat climbing my face betrays me. My thoughts are spiraling wildly, every nerve in my body seeming to betray my better judgment.

Why on earth is my mind entertaining such inappropriate thoughts about a total stranger, one who already feels like an absolute pain? *It's probably just the exhaustion from traveling,* I tell myself. But even as I try to rein in my thoughts, I can feel my irritation brewing.

I don't even know his name yet, but somehow, I already know one thing for sure, I'm going to argue with him, and I'm going to enjoy every second of it.

"Excuse me?" I reply, feeling irritation rising.

"I'm Alex," he introduces himself, ignoring my tone. "If you want to survive here, I suggest you leave those stilts in your suitcase."

Before I can respond, another guy intervenes.

"Don't mind him. Alex doesn't know how to behave. I'm Chris, Val's boyfriend. Welcome!"

I smile weakly, grateful for the interruption. In the following minutes, I'm overwhelmed by a sea of names and faces. Fran, Diego, Aurora... all so welcoming, so different from the anonymous crowd I'm used to. After the energy of the group of young people, Maria, my father's future wife, welcomes me with her usual kindness and hyperactivity that reminds me of her older daughter, Valentina, or Val, as they apparently call her.

"Come, I'll show you your room, you must be tired," says Val, taking me by the arm after all the introductions... which will take me a lifetime to remember.

As we head toward the house, I find myself standing next to Alex, who's almost blocking the entrance. Val says something to him, but I don't hear a word because I'm too distracted.

He shifts slightly, but not enough to avoid brushing against me as I try to follow Val.

"Hey, Rosie," he says softly, so close I can almost feel his warm breath on my skin. What I do feel very clearly, though, is the way he says my name, irritatingly sexy in a way that makes it hard for me to breathe properly. "Are you sure you don't want to go for a horseback ride? It might help you relax. That is, if you can ride, of course."

I also catch the scent of him, and despite his worn clothes, he doesn't smell bad. In fact... I discover, with some horror, that I actually like the way he smells.

Leather and pine.

Of course, I can't seem to come up with a response. I just shoot him the most cowboycidal look I can manage.

Damn it... what's wrong with you, Rosie? You're not that kind of girl!

Despite my mental scolding and my irritation at Alex fucking cowboy, I can't help but notice how the setting sun lights up his hair, casting an almost... *no, Rosie, focus!*

I enter the house while wondering how I'll survive this summer. The feeling from before returns, and I can't help but think that this earthly paradise and that annoying guy with muddy boots have just disrupted my perfectly organized world.

Summer has just begun, and with it, a new adventure that I'm not yet ready to face. I'm not the adventurous type. I'm the type who needs routine and to keep everything under control. Yet, somewhere deep inside me... I like this place. Somewhere inside me, I feel electrified, intrigued, curious... all emotions that I'm not used to feeling and that I probably don't even know how to truly recognize... so I take all these thoughts and lock them away neatly in a corner in the antechamber of my brain. It's easier to feel irritation than to ask too many complicated questions.

My room is small but cozy, with a large window overlooking the fields. I hear the chirping of birds and the rustle of wind through the trees. But above all, I hear the incessant song of cicadas. *Careful not to break an ankle*, I mutter to myself, finally taking off my heels and massaging my sore feet.

Who does he think he is? I can't believe I ever thought he was attractive.

It might help you relax. That is, if you can ride, of course

Ugh. So irritating. So smug. So obnoxious.

I decide not to waste another thought on him, but I promise myself that next time, I'll have a sharp comeback ready.

It's going to be a hellish few months.

I close my eyes and let the exhaustion take over.

Alex

I step back, but I can't resist taking one last glance at Rosie. My heart nearly skipped a beat when she got out of the car. Who would have guessed Robert had such a sexy daughter?

Seriously, this girl doesn't even seem real. With that cascade of red waves, those big brown eyes, her little upturned nose dusted with freckles, and those full lips... lips I'd better not think about.

But trying not to think about her lips, my mind goes straight to her body.

Damn! What made her think it was a good idea to dress like that on a ranch? That ass wrapped in that tight skirt is mouthwatering. And that white blouse? I could pop those buttons off in a second.

Damn it! I almost disgust myself.

Since when do I think about colleagues' daughters like this? And since when do fancy girls turn me on? Damn, it pisses me off! She's so out of place here with her trendy clothes and refined manners. The contrast with the rustic ranch environment is obvious, and I couldn't help but crack that joke. The annoyed look she gave me was... damn exciting!

Wait... why am I moving away? I make another stupid decision and place myself near the front door, knowing Rosie will pass by soon. I don't know what's come over me with this redhead.

I don't know why, but there's an odd pleasure in teasing her... even though I don't even know her.

"Are you already embarrassing our guest?" Val asks, stopping me and walking up with an amused smile and raised eyebrow. Rosie is trailing behind her, of course... in those ridiculous shoes.

"Just a little harmless fun," I reply, raising my hands in surrender, but mentally plotting to drive her crazy.

Drive her crazy?! Now that thought's taking me down a dangerous path... no, best not to think about that. She's definitely not my type. And I'm pretty sure I'm not hers. Not even close. And I still can't figure out why my mind keeps wandering about this redhead I don't even know. I've literally just seen her.

Valentina shakes her head, laughing. "Alex, sometimes you're really just a big kid."

I turn to look at Rosie, flash a grin, and wink at her. The fiery look she gives me is intense. I'm really getting under her skin... and I like it.

Rosie's trying hard to look relaxed, but I notice the tension in her eyes. Her movements are stiff, and she's scanning the place, almost like she's trying to figure out where she is and how to fit in.

A sly smile creeps up on my lips as I realize I really do enjoy poking at Rosie, getting under her skin a little. It's a way to shake her out of her stiff, perfectionist attitude. There's something irresistibly fun about watching her try to keep control while I work to push her out of her comfort zone.

This is going to be one hell of a summer...

For professional reasons, I can't help but analyze every little gesture and movement. And this little princess isn't being honest. The short, clipped answers and forced smiles tell me she's hiding something, maybe a side of herself she doesn't want to show. It's like there's an internal battle going on between the Rosie who's used to LA and the one she could discover here, in this remote ranch. I wonder what she's trying to protect and why she seems so determined to keep control.

My musings could be entirely wrong, though, because I'm totally distracted by that damn redhead walking past just now, way too close, Because, being the massive dickhead that I am, I didn't give her enough space. And I've got to figure out how to not show everyone the damn erection I'm sporting right now.

Especially with Robert, her dad, not too far away.

As I try to mentally scold myself and compose myself... my voice just slips out on its own. Well done, brain-mouth coordination!

"Hey, Rosie," I say, stepping closer with a sly grin. "You sure you don't want to take a ride? It might help you relax a bit... that is, if you know how to ride."

She shoots me a deadly glare, but I see a spark of challenge in her eyes.

Perfect.

Exactly what I was hoping for. There's something thrilling about going toe-to-toe with someone so stubborn. Now I really need to get out of sight and do something about this... situation.

The day ends without further incident, but Rosie continues to occupy my thoughts. There's something about her that challenges me, provokes me, and definitely excites me WAY too much. One thing's for sure, though: this summer is not going to be boring.

Get your copy of *Saddle and Bound* now and keep reading!

Unmasked

Prologue

The air in the hallway hangs heavy, dense and unmoving, as if suspended between reality and the inevitable. Here, far from the buzz of the floors below, every sound is a hushed whisper. Each step I take on the plush velvet feels deliberate, an unspoken call, a note in the prelude of something unknown. My breathing is steady, controlled, but my heart pounds wildly, like the frantic wings of a caged swan, desperate and relentless, echoing off the shadowed walls.

The corset around my waist is a vice, not just shaping me but whispering who I am tonight—or perhaps who I wish to be.

The mask I wear is my answer. Black as onyx, adorned with sleek feathers fanning out like delicate wings, it clings to my face, leaving only my lips bare, a crimson flame in the sea of dark.

It hides me, yet it frees me.

My dress moves with me, as alive as I feel tonight. Soft feathers skim over my chest and meld into a sheer interplay of fabric that stretches down my arms and waist, a second skin. The short, flirty skirt sways with each step, scandalously daring, far too bold.

A black swan, poised between seduction and destruction, woven into every thread of the fabric clinging to my body.

The corridor's dim light pulses faintly ahead, a crimson glow, like the heartbeat of something dark and alive. It guides me, leading me closer to what waits beyond. Every step feels fated, every turn preordained, as though I'm dancing to a script I've never read but somehow already know. My breaths deepen, a tremor sneaking in as I near the door left slightly ajar.

I push it open gently. The room inside is cloaked in shadow, its walls wrapped in velvet that swallows all sound. The red light is a slow, deliberate pulse, stretching across the floor like liquid fire, casting long, flickering shadows.

And there he is, standing.

His suit is ink-black, swallowing the light, turning it to rippling darkness that clings to him. The silver mask obscures his face, fractured in geometric edges that distort what little I can see. His eyes remain hidden, but I feel his gaze as if it's carved into me—sharp and penetrating, like the blade of a knife.

We do not speak. That is the rule. The unspoken pact.

The silence becomes a third presence, amplifying everything our bodies scream without words.

I take a step closer, my heels breaking the silence with rhythmic defiance. Each sound echoes against the velvet stillness, matching the steady pull between us. I stop just steps away, and for a moment, the world halts. The only sounds are our breaths, slow, deep, synchronized.

Then he moves.

It's slow, almost predatory. His hands rise to meet my shoulders, fingers brushing the edges of the feathers there. They trail down my arms, firm yet unhurried, pausing where my corset grips my waist. A shiver runs through me, impossible to hide.

He feels it; I can tell.

Like Odette surrendering to Rothbart's spell, I yield.

His hands tighten, drawing me closer. The scent of his skin, warm and rich, invades my senses. For a moment, our masks graze, a fleeting touch of cold metal against metal, sending a shock through me. The tension we've built shatters, replaced by something consuming and undeniable.

His lips find my neck, warm and soft, leaving a kiss that lingers just long enough to make me ache. Then he bites enough to send a sharp pulse of sensation racing down my spine, a wave of sensation that melds pain and pleasure into a perfect dance.

His hands glide down my back, loosening the corset just enough. The feathers quiver as my body tightens in response.

With practiced ease, he shifts the corset lower, freeing my small breasts. I let go, my thoughts dissolving into the heat of his presence.

He traces my nipples with his fingertips, cupping my left breast with a reverence that feels like worship.

Tonight, I am beauty incarnate, perfection embodied.

A black swan.

He explores my body with a quiet intensity, his hands mapping every curve as though learning me by heart. Each touch sets fire to my skin, every motion deliberate, a slow crescendo that builds to something I can't contain.

When his lips finally claim my breast, they leave trails of heat, drawing an invisible path only he knows. The room fades away; there is only us, our bodies entangled in the soft, flickering crimson light. The world beyond is forgotten, and this moment becomes our stage.

His hands grip my hips, his breath mingling with mine as my dress falls away, piece by piece, leaving nothing but scattered feathers on the floor and my bare body pressed to his.

Every touch is measured, every move agonizingly slow, almost cruel in its restraint. Our masks brush again as his lips claim mine, but the cold metal cannot temper the fire consuming us. My hands find the edges of his suit, pushing it aside to reveal the warmth beneath. Every layer I strip away feels like another step away from control.

Our bodies meet in the semi-darkness, where every sound is absorbed by velvet and crimson light.

He guides me and gently lays me down on the soft, plush bed.

The faint rustle of a condom is the only reminder of reality before he presses against me. He teases, retreats, then enters with a single, forceful thrust, reigniting the shivers and sparks of his bite, but magnified.

I thought tonight might be my rebirth, but it feels more like the swan's final act, a death so blissful, so perfect, I know nothing else will ever compare.

Every movement is a crescendo, every breath a fragment of passion spilling over. With each motion, I surrender a piece of my soul to this stranger. Time vanishes; the outside world ceases to exist.

Then, as we collapse, breathless and entwined, his hand lifts toward my mask. He pauses, giving me a choice.

This is not part of the pact.

I hesitate. My eyes seek his, but they remain hidden in shadow. I take a deep breath, then nod.

His fingers move slowly, lifting the onyx mask from my face. Cold air rushes in, and with it, the truth.

He freezes. He looks at me as if he's seen a ghost.

In turn, my hands reach for his silver mask. My fingers tremble as I remove it, deliberate and final. When his features emerge in the crimson glow, my heart skips a beat.

It's not a stranger. It's him.

His name forms on my lips, but I don't say it. The eyes staring back at me are filled with shock, confusion and guilt.

We've gone too far. The feathers scattered on the floor can never be gathered again. The dance is over, and the lake is deep.

I don't wait for him to speak. Grabbing my clothes with shaking hands, I flee.

Acknowledgments

I want to extend a heartfelt thank you to my first readers.

A special thanks to my Bookstagram friends who have continuously encouraged me and asked for updates. Your support, advice, and enthusiasm have meant the world to me. None of this would have been possible without you.

Thank you to my partner; I never believed in love until I met you.And to my family, thank you for always believing in me and supporting every project I undertake. Your unwavering faith in me has been my anchor.

Printed in Great Britain
by Amazon